HIKE

PETE OSWALD

MEOW!

ZIP!

CLICK!

BLACK BEAR

MUNCH!

KNOCK!
KNOCK!
KNOCK!

CLICK!

CHEERS!

PURR

TO DAD AND PAPA

Planting trees in a public place is sometimes legal, sometimes not. One good way to plant a tree is through an organization dedicated to increasing forestation. Check out thetreesremember.com or www.nationalforests.org.

First edition 2020

Library of Congress Catalog Card Number 2020901762
ISBN 978-1-5362-0157-4

20 21 22 23 24 LEO 10 9 8 7 6 5 4 3 2

Printed in Heshan, Guangdong, China

This book was hand-lettered.
The illustrations were created digitally.

Candlewick Press
99 Dover Street
Somerville, Massachusetts 02144

visit us at www.candlewick.com